Grieving Hope

Edited by Diane Gottlieb

ELJ Editions, Ltd. is committed to publishing works of quality and integrity. In that spirit, we are proud to offer this work of prose to our readers. The stories, the experiences, and the words are the individual authors' alone. Any true events are portrayed to the best of the individual authors' memory and some names and identifying details have been changed to protect the privacy of the people involved.

ISBN: 978-1-942004-89-9

Library of Congress Control Number: 2025935841

Cover Design by ELJ Editions

ELJ Editions, Ltd.
P.O. Box 815
Washingtonville, NY 10992

www.elj-editions.com

Praise for *Grieving Hope*

Memory breaks against the rocky shores of the present in these brief stories of love, loss, and what endures. *Grieving Hope* is a moving—and vital—record of our times.

   –Sue Mell, author of *Giving Care*

Grieving Hope is a moving and at times fiery take on death, morality, love, and friendship. These five writers tell their unique stories of loss, love, and understanding with evocative and powerful writing. It is brave work.

   –Maureen Aitken, author of *The Patron Saint of Lost Girls*

Five exquisite chapbooks make up *Grieving Hope*. Like the windows of a house, they provide distinct glimpses of the forms grief may take, from yearning's sweetness and the terrible poignancy of too-late to ache's persistence, regret, guilt, and blame. And yet, despite loss's varied guise across these pieces, its aspects invariably ring true. They're familiar. Perhaps that is why this collection proves so moving. The reader can recognize its ragged feelings: shapeshifting grief, gnawing missing. The hurt that haunts. The lastingness of sorrow.

   –Melissa Ostrom, author of *Unleaving*

Grieving Hope is a journey into loss. We see families split, relationships broken, a ravished planet, the dementia-induced dissolution of a mind, and the attempted erasure of a culture. These journeys are painful, yet there is also shine in the crisp prose. And, yes, there is hope too. One piece ends: *And try befriending hope and happiness. And keep writing too.* Read this collection and seek out more from these extraordinary writers.

   –François Bereaud, author of *San Diego Stories*

This anthology of five powerful chapbooks explores the delicate threads of memory, loss, and transformation. Through raw honesty and evocative prose, each author invites us to reflect on the moments that shape us, from childhood innocence to the painful reckonings of adulthood. *Grieving Hope* is a moving exploration of the weight and beauty of the past and how we find healing in its echoes.

–Casey Mulligan Walsh, author of *The Full Catastrophe: All I Ever Wanted, Everything I Feared*

Grieving Hope is a lyric exploration of how we survive and who we become after parts of us have been taken away. The five authors of this chapbook have created deftly drawn, sensory worlds of longing; an homage to what can no longer be. This collection honors absence for the shape it leaves within us, wraps the reader in words that pulse and ignite, and illuminates our most solitary moments.

–Ronit Plank, author of *When She Comes Back*

Grief is unpredictable; it comes in many shapes and leaves permanent marks. In its face, hope is almost an act of rebellion. Yet hope germinates within the cracks inflicted by grief. *Grieving Hope* is a brave reminder that the human experience is incomplete otherwise. Each writer succinctly explores grief through narratives that feel personal. The reader is left with several emotions and the aftertaste of hope. In a world causing grief in more ways than one, when Andy Dufresne's words from The Shawshank Redemption about hope being "maybe the best of things" begin to fade from collective memory, may Grieving Hope reignite the beacon for those still lost at sea.

–Tejaswinee Roychowdhury and Ankit Raj Ojha, Editors, *The Hooghly Review*

Table of Contents

PREPARING TO BE WRECKED by Ronita Chattopadhyay

MEMORY'S EBB by Kristina Tabor

THE DOCTOR by Janet Murie

Introduction

When Ariana Den Bleyker asked me to edit *Grieving Hope*, a volume of five micro-chapbooks, I was thrilled—and deeply intrigued. I loved the sound of "grieving hope," the way the words flowed one into the other, the unlikely, but wonderful, juxtaposition. I also wondered what exactly the title meant. Does grieving hope mean that hope is lost and we are in the process of mourning that loss? Does the fact that grief exists—that people allow themselves to engage with that powerful and very difficult emotion—bring on hope? I sensed the two words were connected in important ways but was curious about how people hold both grief and hope at the same time. How would they express both on the page?

I was surprised by the range of emotions I felt while reading these micro-chapbooks exploring grief. Of course, I expected to be moved; I was prepared for these singular grief experiences to touch my own and speak to the universal. What I hadn't anticipated was how the quiet thread of hope, binding these stories together, was what most deeply connected me to the words, the stories, and to the beautiful voices that tell them.

In Charlotte Hamrick's lusciously lyrical *Offset Melodies*, we follow a young girl as she travels from childhood into adolescence and into young adulthood, as told through the lens of a wise adult woman looking back. The micro-chapbook sings with powerful images of time and place, nature, nurture, and the disillusionments and disappointments of living and growing in an imperfect world populated by imperfect people. There are memories alongside reality, family and friends, running and being left, holding on and letting go. There is pain. There is grief. And, always, the narrator moves forward; she falls, she gets up, she learns, and she grows. "All my experiences collect, filling my cracked cup. I hold it tight between my finger bones." Life. Love. Grief. Hope.

Kim Steutermann Rogers writes of environmental, animal, and human loss in *Denatured: Stories of Change* through stories that intertwine all of the above. There is the grief of losing a beloved dog, a seal, the precious 'akikiki.

There is human loss, too—a marriage, infertility, substance abuse. In each of the stories, Rogers examines the relationships between humans and animals—and humans and mangoes. The result is a unique collection that will not only make you feel but make you think. Rogers experiments with form. In "Animal Nature" we are treated to the "thoughts" and experience of an elder pig; in "A Kindness of Ravens" we learn of how ravens, on several occasions, saved a character's life. In "Things Washed Ashore When the Whales Went Extinct," Rogers lists item upon item that pollute the oceans and might someday be responsible for the extinction of whales. While Rogers shares how humans are culpable, she also writes movingly about how people work to save the environment, how the environment saves us, and how we save what we can in each other.

In *Preparing to Get Wrecked*, Ronita Chattopadhyay examines the power of "that first loss," the one that changes our lives and colors the way we view losses to come. The narrator's first deeply felt loss is a complicated one—the death of a childhood friend by accidental drowning—that leaves the narrator asking questions she will never be able to answer. "Why"s and "What-if"s swim in gorgeous water imagery. Reminders of the loss are everywhere and in everything, and the narrator wonders how to prepare herself for the inevitable future losses she will experience. Hope breaks through the veil of grief towards the end of the collection. Chattopadhyay offers loving rays of hope in a piece addressed to the "ten-year-old me." She closes out the collection with a poignant reflection on how communion with others who share the same loss helps to keep memory alive.

Kristina Tabor takes us down the heart-breaking path of her mother's dementia in *Memory's Ebb*. Using a quiet, matter-of-fact tone, Tabor provides a stark and startling contrast to her mother's cognitive decline. These are not small losses. Once a fiercely independent woman, Tabor's mother loses the ability to live on her own. She becomes an easy target for scammers; her confusion is terrifying to her and to those who love her; her once vibrant personality, wilts. And she forgets. First, it's where she puts her phone, then how often she sends the same text. She forgets words, forgets how to drive, how to feed herself, how to swallow. Here, still, in Tabor's patience, in the loving care she provides, and in the memories Tabor holds of her mother, whole and "remarkable," hope lives.

Janet Murie's *The Doctor* may be the most difficult read in the volume, as it speaks to a horrific period in Canadian history. Murie sends chills through the reader in her one-sentence opening: "My father was a residential school doctor." What follows is her attempt to piece together information and gain understanding of her early life and the likelihood that her father was paid by the Canadian government to conduct medical experiments on Indigenous people. Murie recently learned there were "96 bodies beneath the property I grew up on that was part of Sto:lo Nation." What does one do with such devastating pieces of knowledge? How does she hold the grief of a painful childhood alongside the great harm perpetrated against a community and a people at the hand of her father and others in her family's circle? Murie moves back and forth between time periods in her life and between her father and her mother in short, stark, beautifully crafted chapters. The hope lies in Murie's quest to uncover and to share what she has discovered, to shine a light on a dark time and her family's place in it, and to find her own way through her family's past.

Grief. Hope. The words are not incongruous. While, at times, one may overshadow the other, both must be present if we are to live full lives. I have learned a great deal from the five gorgeous voices in this volume and have been changed by each of the stories. It is my wish that readers of *Grieving Hope* will have a similar experience. *Grieving Hope* is a small volume of micro-chapbooks, but it is big on wisdom and beauty. It is full of life.

Diane Gottlieb
December 31, 2024

Offset Melodies

Charlotte Hamrick

Polaroid

For ten years you were frozen in a fairy dress. Sweet head of downy hair, lips a perfect O, round eyes and gossamer lashes looking into the camera, tiny feet in pristine white.

Behind us, a hill in full flora. Sun shining as though every day of us would last forever. We didn't know our forever would be kidnapped, our every days destroyed by parents more childish than we.

Memory Rooms

The house in my head is as snug against a hill as two sisters spooning at nap time, has a field of wild tiger lilies with smiley-bright faces, and a sparkling creek where minnows swim, tiny wiggly uncut jewels.

The house in my head has blue morning glories where fairies play entwined around a small porch leading into the kitchen. The scent of freshly baked bread wafts through the door like a warm hug in soft arms.

The house in my head has a washing machine in the basement that dances, a wondrous thing where colors and patterns jiggle up & down like trapeze artists, where an affectionate voice cautions my curious impulses.

The house in my head is like a dream but a not-dream. It was long ago but just yesterday. In that house trouble and fear didn't exist. Now when trouble finds me, I float through my memory rooms, sit at the old kitchen table for bread and jam, peek at the dancing colors in the washing machine, then lie down in my cozy bed at the top of the stairs where I'm not afraid of the monster underneath because even it is kind.

Carolina

It happened like this. The babies were put to bed, and we were shooed out of the house so the grownups could dance to Patsy Cline or Connie Smith or Jim Reeves and drink beer on long, hot Carolina evenings. Daddies looked cool in civvies, their fatigues hanging stiff on clotheslines, and mammas looked mod in pastel pedal-pushers and sleeveless tops, hair piled high in what was called a beehive. But we never did see any bees up there. We would play stoop tag or draw cartoons in the front yard dirt until we got bored. We lived on a dead-end street and all the action was up the hill on Scarborough where teenagers cruised looking for excitement on summer nights, the guys in hopped up Chevy's and the girls in their mamma's station wagons. Me and Billy and Juanita ached to walk up to the stop sign to closer watch the passing cars. We liked to think up stories for tired-looking people that were probably only driving to the grocery store or back home after work. We gave them more exotic and dangerous lives in our stories, making them spies like Jim and Cinnamon in Mission Impossible or Star Trek crew members tracking Klingons. But we never did walk all the way up to Scarborough because we knew our daddies would tan our hides. We'd just sit outside the house, listening to the music and laughter until somebody punched somebody else and we'd finally see some action.

Anyway, that's how I remember it.

Offset Melodies

Each morning stretches hot and indifferent. The girl works in the vegetable garden among the runner bean plants, twining the pliant tendrils around bean poles. The newly born plants that emerged from dry brown seeds are flexible and soft in her hands. The heart-shaped leaves hum as she works, hum heart-shaped songs or songs that shape hearts. All the girl knows about hearts is that hers is still and dry as a stone vessel waiting to be filled.

§

Once, the girl's heart was alive with curiosity, flowers, and freedom, embraced by never-ending story-time, twilight sing-a-longs, and hands that always gave. It becomes harder to remember the soaring joy of her once-filled heart, to believe it will ever be filled again.

§

Each morning's blooms of bejeweled red ruffles wave at the girl-in-waiting, at her poor dry heart-in-waiting. The flowers whisper words that mingle with the humming heart-shaped leaves, whisper *waiting is good practice for fulfilling.* The girl rubs her thumbs over the sun soaked leaves, feels hundreds of vibrating hearts humming together. Deeper still, she feels a mother-thrumming from the furrowed earth that birthed the bean plants, that birthed every plant since the Big Bang.

§

Mothers are made, not born. They are a want-to-be, not a given.

§

Each morning she watches as the bean pods flourish, she *rub rub rubs* them between her fingers and thumb, feels their growing fullness, tends the twining vines. How they whisper and hum in her hands...

§

You're the only one our hearts beat for

§

Flutter....... goes her heart.

Besties at the Beach

Rummaging through an old box of ephemera, I spied the curled edges of an old photo in fading gray and white...
Summer.
Ocean.

The two of us in mid-run.

You were already showing a slender c-curve waist to hips, I was thick-waisted with baby fat. And my thighs...
Dimpled.
Doughy.

My chunky body forever running down a pier, arms akimbo, hair frozen in an upward thrust. You by my side...
Gazelle-like.
Graceful.

First trip to the ocean, first real swimsuit, and the first time I remember comparing my body to another. A snapshot in time of joy as I ran toward the sparkling ocean next to you, my best friend, and envy for your emerging womanly curves.

Fly Like a Kite

Then one day you dropped out of school and decided to join the army. You started talking about how we could run away and get married, travel the world. You said that you'd love me forever. One afternoon you picked me up and said *Today is the day*, just like that, like I didn't have a say in the matter. I looked out the car window and saw a red and yellow kite riding the air currents free, untethered, and beautifully independent. I told you I was too young to get married. Even at 16, I knew forever was longer than my attention span.

Water Magic

Baptized in early spring sunlight, nursing an ache for anarchy, we skipped school - hiding in Susan's car until the morning bell blew. Feeling brave and daring (the kind of girls who skipped school!) we drove ourselves *outa there*, the lake pulling us like the moon pulls the tides. We banana-peeled off our clothes then raced to the lake's edge, plunging into the Spring-cold surface, nimble Naiads all arms and legs and tossing hair, reveling in watery abandon. We felt weightless, carefree, flinging out our daring arms, releasing our anvil of teenage angst. How glorious it felt to be away from disapproving adult eyes, free from expectations, to be independent and invisible with only the winking lake to see us.

Smoke on the Midway

Our last year together felt like your beloved game of chess, the board of us nestled nonchalantly under your arm one day, stuffed in your locker the next, kings and queens rolling against each other in repose waiting for the interlocking of fingers.

You were a tire swing launched over a river of turbulent waters, swaying from side to side. Landing on my bank one week, on hers another.

She was Elton John, piano lessons, only child, 16th birthday new car, college prep classes.

I was Led Zeppelin, headphone drums, oldest child, bummer of rides, part-time shelf stocker.

She was a smooth still lake, I was a house on fire.

It was me you took to the carnival, sounds of hurly-burly music and crow calls of the barkers weaving through a murmuration of bodies in the midway. She would have shrunk away from the musk, the sweat, the proximity of flesh. I imagined her wrinkled forehead, hand over mouth. To me the carnival was exotic, the restlessness of the crowds a high, its travelers living an enviable freedom.

You knew this about her, about me.

I lost you that night when you lost your leather fringed jacket, a prized possession, to the carnival barker, a trade for another try at a stuffed animal I didn't want. You shivered in the cold November air, one step ahead as we walked back to your car.

Your daddy bought back the jacket. I saw you wearing it a few days later, your arm around her.

You left me behind, a lingering smoke, a house burned down.

Bus Ticket

The bus doors closed with a squeak and a *whoosh*. The cloud of her hair drifted down the aisle, settling in a window.

This is how I imagined it the afternoon Deanie made good on her decision to run away. I had decided to stay behind but had a hand in the logistics of her flight. I stood behind the counter in the drugstore where I worked, dusting shelves while watching for the 2:15 bus I knew would pass on the street outside, never believing she'd actually go through with it.

I'd lent my car to her for the drive to the bus station so when my co-worker dropped me off there after work, I expected my keys to be hidden under the seat. They were not. I was stranded with no choice but to call my mom. I had planned to keep her secret, but I was never a good liar.

Truth is, I didn't even ask where her ticket would take her. I was holding onto the hope that she'd drive up at quitting time when we'd go to the Sonic, order our customary chili cheese dog and tater tots, and continue the thread of our small-town trajectory.

For years after I thought of her almost every day.

Sometimes I imagined she was living the different kind of life she wanted, happy and carefree.

Sometimes I imagined she was married with little cotton-headed children.

Sometimes - and this scared the hell out of me - I imagined she was living on the streets but too proud to call for help.

Mostly, though, I thought about our bond of not-fitting-in and the times we held each other up in the laughing and the crying. Now only memories.

Chili cheese dogs and tater tots never tasted the same again.

Pine Trees & Kudzu

Marinating in a rooted town where no one ever left & nothing changed, I waited, eyes bright with taillights, for my day of escape. In the arc of sleepless nights, I'd sometimes catch the Jackson frequency, hear "Born to Run," feel a bright wild jet stream run through my veins, wings thrumming beneath my skin, a long, hard stretch toward something besides pine trees & kudzu, besides cruising Main Street & parking at The Lake.

Years bloomed with the passing of time; miles stretched longer than 63,360 inches while time shortened to a *snap!* - the people & places of my past grew tiny as cities viewed from a jetliner. Now, sleepless nights are ghost-filled rooms I walk in my mind. Sometimes homesickness passes through, a storm front of pine trees shaking everything I ran from.

Pathways

I was never the girl who knew what she wanted and expected nothing less or the one who walked with a confident air, flipping her long silken hair over her shoulder, flashing a smile the brightness of a dentist's fantasy.

I was never the girl who could speak with ease about Beat poets or the literati or debate the social relevance of some obscure '70's Punk band.

I was never the girl with the perfect Southern manners who kept her ankles crossed, had the perfect manicure and never a stray brow out of place.

I was the girl who loved the sparkle of the stars in an inky night sky, beaconing Morse code from the heart of the universe, although I could never remember their names or the constellations they lived in.

I was the girl who loved The Blues, the earnest, heart-aching want that reached out of the radio grabbing me by the throat where the beat of my pulse thumped like a wild thing in harmony with those who wrote such tormented words with the blood of their loss.

I was the girl who loved the written word that took me to places I could only imagine. Exotic cultures and lush landscapes were the companions of my daydreamy world.

I was the girl who walked barefoot through the woods with the red dust of Mississippi between her toes and long lonely days to contemplate How Things Are and How Things Might Be.

I am the woman who changed How Things Were and became who I wanted to be.

Days Come 'Round

All I know of love and life has settled in my bones. Days and years of trial and error, of doing my best and worst, of getting out of bed then falling back in.

All the hours in between rode bareback in faith or stupidity, the what-ifs or how-longs leaned on hope.

All my experiences collect, filling my cracked cup. I hold it tight between my finger bones. It's all that I know.

Acknowledgments

Many thanks to the literary journals that first published the following:

Polaroid in *The Citron Review.*

Offset Melodies in *Louisiana Literature.*

Smoke on the Midway in *Trampset.*

Pine Trees & Kudzu in *Hobo Camp Review.*

About the Author

Charlotte Hamrick began writing at age 53 after retiring from the healthcare field. She has been published in a number of literary journals including *Still: The Journal*, *The Citron Review*, *Atticus Review*, *Louisiana Literature*, and her work is included in *Best Small Fictions 2022* and *2023*. She's had multiple literary nominations for her Flash Fiction and Poetry and her Creative Nonfiction was a finalist for the 15th Glass Woman Prize. She is Managing Editor for *Reckon Review*. She lives in New Orleans with her husband and a menagerie of rescued pets.

Denatured: Stories of Change

Kim Steutermann Rogers

I.

Do You Believe in Miracles?

It was the night the U.S. Olympic hockey team beat four-time defending gold medalists, the Soviet Union. Height of the Cold War, 1980. I gave Missy her meds and let her outside before bed. Temperatures hovered at 40 degrees, warm for February in Chicago. Missy, our graying 14-year-old standard poodle, was epileptic, a little arthritic, too, and taking longer to do her business. After years of trying to get pregnant and not, we looked to Missy to make our marriage a family, silly as that may sound. We had a routine: I let Missy out, and fifteen minutes later, Jeff would let her in.

At 10:00, the entire 30-minute newscast covered what *Sports Illustrated* would dub the Miracle on Ice. The team's youth. The Soviet Union's dominance, a roster, for all intents and purposes, made up of professional players. You know how America loves an underdog.

I got caught up in it, too. The U.S. was ahead 4 - 3. Growing up hiding under school desks in case of a nuclear attack, every American, hockey fan or not, couldn't help but jump up and down in front of their living room Magnavox at the potential victory. David conquering Goliath. We were solid then, Jeff and me.

With 33 seconds on the clock, the Soviets fired a slap shot and the U.S. goalie somehow defended it. But the Soviets recovered the puck—now, 20 seconds left—and sent in another shot. A miss. The U.S. team cleared the puck and sportscaster Al Michaels counted down the clock, delivering his famous call. "Five seconds left in the game. Do you believe in miracles? Yes!"

When we remembered the dog, Jeff went to the back door, and she wasn't there. We got the call from the police more than a week later—after we'd stopped driving the streets, after we'd stopped posting flyers, after we'd stopped crying her name.

I'm not saying our marriage ended that night, but a little part of my heart iced over and cracked when I drove to the police station to pick up Missy's collar, my finger stroking the black leather studded with rhinestones, all but three missing.

Science Lesson

The night after we killed the seal, I ate pork and beans for dinner, right out of the can. The seal was endangered, in the prime of his life, his death a terrible accident. Ben went to his tent. I went to mine. Sleep didn't come. I got up and walked down to the water's edge where the seal had died. With no moon overhead, the Milky Way's zillion stars lit up the sky. We had injected the seal with a sedative, a heavy dose, sure, but well within the safe range for his big size. The objective had been to take his measurements—length from nose to tail and girth around the belly below his pectoral fins—and collect blood, skin, saliva, and fecal samples. Then, pierce his rear flipper and slide in a plastic tag with a unique ID number, enabling us to track him throughout his life. It wasn't a risky procedure. We'd done it many times that summer.

"Have you ever killed a seal before?" Ben asked before he turned in.

I hadn't. This was my first field season.

We had approached him on the sand from behind, using a hoop net to catch him. It didn't take much wrangling before the sedative took effect, and he settled down. The seal had been so close to entering the sea and diving to depths of three and five hundred feet to nose around for lobsters and eels hidden in the crevices of coral and under rocks, using an adaptive technique evolved over millions of years to stay submerged, slowing his heart rate to single digits per minute, something called bradycardia.

"We didn't do anything wrong." Ben said. "It happens. Sometimes."

I was supposed to watch his respirations, count his breaths, and I did. But seals are good at camouflaging their inhalations and exhalations. I wasn't sure when he took his last breath. It was Ben who first realized something was wrong. He lifted the seal's muzzle and slapped his nose, pinched the skin between the bones of his fore-flipper to trigger a startle reflex, injected him with a reversal drug, stuck him with epinephrine, intubated him, pumped air into his chest, anything to pull him back from the deepest dive of his life.

It wasn't until Ben pulled out his stethoscope, placed it on the seal's side, then sat back on his heels, wrapped the scope around his neck like doctors do, and shook his head that I got it. In saving seals, you sometimes lose them.

"I lost one years ago," Ben said before he went to sleep. "I'll never forget it."

No waves broke inside the lagoon, stars sizzling on its surface. I followed the seal's trail in reverse, from the ocean's edge where he'd died to the spot on the beach he'd left hours before, his sleeping pit, where he'd wriggled and rested and rolled around during the last night of his life. I crawled inside the sandy pit, curled in a ball, catching musky whiffs of wild seal whenever the land breeze blew.

Birdfall

Thirty years later, when they're together again—all except Jackson—they'll say it happened the summer of record heat waves. The summer warming temperatures saw mosquitoes infected with avian malaria march up knife-edged mountains, and the last of the rare birds fell from the sky.

The two old-timers will have gathered at the invitation of a young brood of scientists hoping to resurrect the lost birds of Hawai'i using DNA from museum skins to re-wild the forest.

What was it like to hear 'i'iwi in the forest? an eager-faced ornithologist will ask.

Maile, who left science for a 9-to-5 insurance job in Honolulu, was the last to hear the vermilion-bodied bird with a salmon-colored bill the shape and length of a fishhook. The sun was cresting Mt. Wai'ale'ale, she'll say, when she heard the tell-tale sound of a rusty gate and jolted awake. She'll say the bird was once so plentiful its feathers wrapped the shoulders of her ancestors.

What was the 'anianiau like in real life?

Taylor had traded endangered Hawaiian forest birds for invasive barn owl control on the continent. He'll say the honeycreeper was the color of the sun itself and the "cutest little fuzzball you ever saw."

What about 'akikiki?

Maile will look at Taylor. Neither will say 'akikiki was Jackson's favorite bird. That Jackson liked it for the very reason it was so easily overlooked. Not charismatic red or yellow but pale gray. Not a high-flying nectar feeder but enigmatic, creeping up and down tree trunks in search of grubs. Neither will mention next month marks the 30th year of Jackson's manslaughter sentence.

We've heard stories of heroism, how you tried to save them.

Maile will say they patched together extension ladders 100-feet in the air to rescue orphans, a failed effort to raise chicks in captivity.

Neither will mention the story might have had a different ending if Mosquitoes Matter hadn't roadblocked Jackson's pioneering project to eliminate the swarms of disease-carrying mosquitoes sweeping up the mountain. How close they were to saving the last of the rare birds found in Hawai'i and nowhere else in the world.

Eventually, the eager young scientists will leave, confident their science will resurrect Hawaii's lost birds. Maile and Taylor will stick around. Maile will mention their last night in camp those many years ago. Taylor will say it was Carrot who pushed Jackson over the edge. Carrot the 'akikiki Jackson named for the two orange-colored bands he'd circled around the bird's leg, their way of identifying individuals. How Jackson had been monitoring Carrot for seven years until one day the honeycreeper fell dead from the sky and—this is the truth—landed in Jackson's lap, a mosquito still sucking the bird's blood.

"If you had it to do over again," Maile starts.

"I'd say Jackson was with us the whole night the science deniers fell off the cliff."

Maile nods. "That the forest is a precipitous place unless you know exactly where to step."

Things Washed Ashore When the Whales Went Extinct

- Plastic beverage bottles and caps, detached from each other and the lips that drained them.

- Plastic toothbrushes, bristles rubbed off.

- Cigarette butts and plastic Bic lighters, encased in the smoky breath of climate deniers, ribboning across the high tide line.

- Plastic forks, tines missing like the last known scientist at the last field station in the middle of the Pacific Ocean.

- Seabird skeleton noosed with a string attached to a deflated mylar balloon, the only letters readable: H A P_Y B I R___ A Y.

- Plastic drink lids with the "diet" symbol, like hope, depressed.

- Fishing nets, fishing lines, fishing floats.

- Crabless shells and meatless mollusks, all chipped and cracked like someone's Grandma's china.

- Red-and-yellow-striped plastic straws, drained from inland rivers and streams.

- A line of green plastic stir sticks embossed with a mermaid logo.

- Toddler-sized Crocs in a rainbow of colors, Hello Kitty charms still intact.

- Plastic grocery bags nested inside the carapace of a sea turtle.

- Shattered corpse of a cell phone, its face reflecting fractured rays from a relentless sun.

- Brittle plastic laundry baskets and plastic laundry detergent jugs, breaking into shards of a jigsaw puzzle.

- Outsoles of athletic shoes, pocked and pitted and dimpled.

- Canopy of fake tree from a cell phone tower.

- A fishing skiff, minus motor and catch and life.

- String of fabric prayer flags, frayed and faded.

- Plastic five-gallon bucket, still lidded, filled with a dozen packets of dehydrated Mountain House Creamy Macaroni & Cheese.

- Waves tickling the feet of a human body, desiccated, long hair attached, a yellow Rite-in-the-Rain notebook embraced, the words in pencil: The End.

Animal Nature

The elder pig with the uniquely straight tail and long anteater-like snout lives in a cabin in the woods at the base of a steep valley. On spring days, he hunkers down in wallows of mud, all alone as the scent of apple blossoms blows downwind and mingles with the song of Northern cardinals freshly released from winter's freeze.

Spring always reminds him of life in the before times when litters of his piglets trailed his heels, when he captained the town's rugby team, and when, admittedly, he made very poor life choices, that long nose of his getting him in trouble. Hubris may have been at play then, but he couldn't resist those exquisitely rare birds—petrels, were they? He nosed his way into their underground burrows and devoured them, bones and all, caching the shiny bangles that circled their skinny bird legs and lining up the bands on his mantel where they sparkled in firelight. He doesn't say he was banished from family, from society. He says he's grown introverted as he's grown older. But truth is, he misses his sow, his streams of straight-tailed, long-nosed piglets.

For years, he manages his penance, sticking to a vegetarian diet, fearful the hunger inside him will vanquish his years of restraint, fearful one misguided snort will lose him his badge. On nights of the full moon, the aging hog saunters through the valley, binging on the exposed roots of hardwoods. He gorges on the first stalks of young rhubarb growing on the well-drained eastern-facing slopes of the valley.

But new moons are always hard. New moons make him restless. His confessor prescribed fifty Hail Marys and fifty Our Fathers to get him through the night. But on the first new moon of his 666th year, neither Mother nor Father can restrain him. He aches to sink his incisors in tender flesh, hear bone crunch between his jaws, and before he can stop himself, he's hoofing it to the village on the ridge. On the way, he has to pause three times to catch his breath tunneling through his long nasal passages. He heads, first, for the stone cottage to see his family before sating himself at the site of his plunder in the before days. It's a stretch, especially now that arthritis has settled and stiffened his spine, but he stands on his hind legs and peers inside the window. It takes a few seconds for his eyes to take in the sight; cataracts have clouded his vision. But he can see well enough to make out curly-tailed piglets and know they are not his descendants. He sees a boar he doesn't know mount his sow, and what he realizes before his heart seizes and his body thumps to the ground, four short legs stick-straight in the air, is his family has gotten on.

It's like he never existed at all.

Salted Watermelon

The woman dropped the watermelon in the parking lot of the Amish country store. Bloody flesh and dark seeds exploded on the ground, matched by a burst of the woman's salty tears that rushed downhill to a patch of straw grass where a rat, taking refuge from the summer heat under an empty box of s'mores granola bars—cardboard faded to tan in the summer sun—lapped up the juice.

The heat. Even the rat, called Red for the tint of his fur, was lethargic, preferring to snooze through nights as well as days, losing a few ounces because he wasn't eating but who didn't need to lose a bit of weight after a long winter and a wet spring.

But this. This salty-sweet, life-saving, blood-red liquid arrived with a parallel taste of something else. Red felt his ribs contract and his breathing catch, as if he'd swallowed a soft bone from a young mouse, hairless, its eyes still shut. Innocent. It was like a boa was constricting Red's head, surfacing memories, the ones he'd planted deep in his hippocampus, one in particular, this one about another baby, his baby, babies, rather, the babies he'd most recently left behind three miles away at an all-night convenience store off I-80 for no good reason other than he was the kind of rat that ran.

Sure, he ran—time and again—but his super power, he liked to think, was his sense of taste, hundreds, maybe thousands more taste buds than your average rat, able to discern and avoid toxins like diphacinone and brodifacoum laid out by the likes of this woman who was now sliding to the ground outside of her Ford Bronco the way tears slid down her face, silently. Yeah, he ran. He ran and spread his DNA and ran again, but he also knew by the taste of the salted watermelon juice that the woman had just done something she said she'd never do, never imagined she'd have to do, never thought in a million years she'd need to seek out a certain doctor who performed procedures after hours, whose offices moved from place to place, here the most unexpected of places, and so Red waited until the woman's tears dried and she pulled herself up and drove off before he ran over and raided the remains of the watermelon rind.

Because Red was not your ordinary rat.

A Kindness of Ravens

It started when the tide ebbed and ravens winged it for the Homer Public Library where Erin and townsfolk flocked in the parking lot, even in foul Alaska weather because Alaskans knew weather was like a cantankerous great aunt who had to be acknowledged but could also be ignored. At noon, everyone doled out food to the resident birds. But this time, the ravens didn't stop at the library. They disappeared over the ridge, and Erin knew what that meant, dropping her French fries and climbing to the roof of the library even before the tsunami alarm rang.

The second time a raven saved her life, Erin was seventeen and foraging for morels in the Cascade Mountains when a whiteout swallowed the hiking trail. Erin knew the most important thing to do was stay positive, so she sang "Shake It Off," the snow dense as blackout curtains, her words hitting a dull reverb, when she made out the shape of a raven with sapphire eyes in flight and followed the breadcrumbs of shiny pennies it dropped all the way back to her SUV.

Over the years, Erin's lost track of the number of ravens that have come to her rescue. Once in an alley outside a bar on Haight Street in San Francisco, a guy she'd throated tequila shots with started getting rough when a siren chirped, causing him to run, and Erin saw a one-legged raven perched on a window ledge. Was that a smirk creasing its beak?

But the kindest thing a raven has ever done for her— standing on the Santa Monica pier having just hung up with her mother's news about her father—is this: a raven sitting a foot away, preening and scratching. A raven just being a raven and allowing her into the moment.

II

Mango Madness

It was morning, the third of my honeymoon, and I headed out for my solo run. From a distance, I saw colorful dots on the road that turned out to be mangoes, fallen and run over by tourists' rental cars. I dodged the meaty pulp on the ground the way I would mud puddles, intent on keeping my regular eight-minute mile pace, when a mango fell, brushing my shoulder and swirling to the ground at my feet, stopping me.

I took it as a sign and picked it up, rubbing its smooth skin to my cheek and catching a sweet scent emoting near the stem's end. Without thinking, I sunk my teeth into the fruit, juice dribbling down my chin, following the curve of my neck down my chest and between my breasts. I looked up into the dense umbrella of slender leaves, staring up at its fruity sunset-colored ripe ornaments. I was in love.

Every morning for the six days left of my honeymoon, I returned to this mango tree, eating one mango after another, handfuls of mangoes, so many mangoes, sure the yellow-orange meat was key to my fertility. When it came time to leave, I slipped a mango pit into my suitcase.

Six weeks later, a stick turned pink. I knew it. Hopeful, I planted the mango pit into the ground. But 33 days after that, I miscarried.

I wanted to try again, but there were no mangoes. It was too soon. It took 10 years for the tree to fruit. By then, there were no more eggs. I watched as green mangoes ripened into sunbursts and fell to the ground, eaten alive by ants and flies. One day, I went outside and gathered a basket of mangoes. I had meant to bury them. Mark their graves with a stone. But their aroma overtook me, and I sat on the ground caressing each mango against my cheek, tears mixing with the oils of the fruit on my face. Soon, my face started burning. My hands, itching.

This time, the oils weeping from the mango ignited oozing blisters on my skin. My throat tightened. My head grew dizzy. I struggled to pull air into my lungs. All that was left for me to do was scratch my heart out.

This Bud's for You

Someone said they never thought Ryan would be first. Someone said he was the only one with a life plan. Someone said thunderstorms can be 15 miles in diameter and last an average of 30 minutes. Someone said remember how Ryan walked the halls singing advertising jingles? Someone started counting *one-Mississippi, two-Mississippi*. Someone said, *Weekends were made for Michelob* was Ryan's favorite. Someone else said Budweiser. Someone got to one-thousand-three before thunder bellowed. Someone suggested meeting at the cave, our favorite high school hangout, even as lightning splintered the sky above the inky river. Someone asked, remember how we pinky-promised to stay in touch?

Alarm

The National Guard bangs on the door at 3:17 a.m. At the same time, your phone rings. You know it's Missy even before the automated voice kicks in saying, *This is a call from a person in Geneva Women's Correctional Facility. If you do not wish to accept this call, please hang up now.*

You do not hang up. When it comes to your sister, you never hang up.

"The house is in the fire path," Missy says, locked up this time for vandalizing bulldozers at a swank new residential development. "Take Virg."

Virg. It's always Virg.

"She's family," Missy says.

Family, Missy said when she first found Virg, rump spotted, trying to suckle a mother whose blood and life oozed from a gunshot wound. Virg short for Virginia, a take off her binomial scientific name—*Odocoileus virginianus*.

Can't abandon family, Missy said five years later, dragging the deer's car-battered carcass home and keening like a cat until Dad agreed to taxidermy Virg.

Family photo, Missy said, demanding we gather around Virg's head every holiday.

On the night of Missy's senior prom, Billy Thompson refused to pose next to Virg, and Missy handed his red carnation wrist corsage back to him, went upstairs, and changed out of her pink taffeta dress. The story made its way through the guy's locker room, as they do, tagging Missy—and you, by extension—as the bat-shit crazy farm kids. Missy asked the next guy if he liked deer, and he said he loved venison. Missy gave up boys on the spot and stuck to it ever since.

Standing at the front door, a man in Army fatigues waves his hand, Missy continues battering your ear, and you can see Virg hanging on the dining room wall of your childhood home, Virg and you the only ones still inhabiting it.

"Gotta go," the guard says, his voice adamant, the smell of smoke pungentating the air.

"Do you think Virg understood what was happening in the glare of the headlights," you ask Missy. "Do you think her tail flashed white?" You hit "end" before Missy can answer and take one last look at Virg as you close the door behind you, note the flames reflecting in the deer's dead eyes.

Fault Lines

I ask myself who is the woman in the smoke lines around your mouth, the woman with the pointy hipbones you didn't get from working out, the woman with the Timber rattler's stare in your golden-brown eyes. I ask myself if I should have stayed home and gone to community college, waited for you to graduate high school. If I should have stopped you from hanging out with the boys outside 7-11, because I knew what they were selling. If I should have told you about our drunk-deserting Dad, me, the only one of us to remember it was like non-stop seismic tremors having him around. I ask myself what happened to my sister who dressed as a unicorn for Halloween three years in a row, who always knew when to release the rope swing at its highest point and go cartwheeling into the calm side channel of the Mississippi River, who made Bs to my Cs. While Mom worked the evening shift at the shoe factory, we ran feral, finger-painting masterpieces with the alluvium constantly getting churned up by the river. We made blanket forts and camped at the epicenter of the earthquake that a hundred years ago shook buildings as far away as St. Louis. We shared *Teen Vogue* and, then, *People* magazines. And, even when I hated you for telling Mom I was sneaking out after curfew, I loved you.

But I know you're stealing money from Mom's checking account. I know you're taking Mom's Vicodin. I know you showed up drunk at Mom's hospice bed, and I blame myself. I blame myself for not protecting you from our family's fault lines. I know there's a 10 percent chance for another large earthquake in the next 50 years. I know the National Institute on Drug Abuse reports three out of four addicts eventually recover. I know my love is stretched thin as a rattler's shed skin.

Cleaning House

*A*cross town, a large hole is being dug to contain your grief, the headline read. Come by at dawn, dump your troubles, start a new day.

The first day, Jen offloaded her ex's favorite coffee mug, the stained one with a big blue "M," the logo of his college alma mater, keeping the blue enamelware cup emblazoned with a cartoonish bird from her community college. The next day, she dumped his drawer of socks, drawer and all, and stopped grinding her teeth at night. Then, their wedding gifts from his family went—the china with tiny blue flowers his mother insisted every young bride needed, his dead grandmother's precious collection of Hummel figurines. Her taste for vegetables—especially his hated asparagus—returned. When she got to the garage, she had to pay a neighbor boy to help with the used refrigerator her ex bought for his craft beer collection. She didn't need an extra refrigerator. She knew what alcohol could do to a family. Her ex drove off in his 1969 restored red Mustang with his new TaylorMade golf set in the trunk, but she offloaded his old irons, forgotten like her and Rex the mutt they'd adopted on their third wedding anniversary.

For five months, Jen continued to show up every day at the gulf in the ground, now hurling the slights he'd directed at her. *There's never anything to eat in this house. Are you wearing that again?* The most painful, *Why can't you get pregnant?*

She stopped chewing the inside of her cheek. The numbness in her feet went away, and she stood her full five-feet-eight-inches. She grew out her mouse-brown hair, leaving the gray uncolored.

Once she'd cleared out his belongings and everything that whispered his presence in her life, the house nearly empty, she painted the walls a fresh coat of celadon green, because the color made her smile again. He would never have approved green because anything but neutral colors would hurt the resale value of the house. She no longer cared about resale values.

It took a full year, 365 days, before she was completely done with him, and she felt fully herself. On that day, she started menstruating again. The next day, she called a wrecking crew, watched as they hoisted the house on a trailer, and she and Rex led them across town.

Acknowledgements

Thank you to the editors of the following publications where these stories first appeared:

"Science Lesson" *The Dodge*

"A Kindness of Ravens" *Flash Flood Journal*

"Mango Madness" *Emerge Literary Journal*

"Cleaning House" *Reckon Review*

About the Author

Kim Steutermann Rogers lives in Hawaii. Her prose has published recently in *Ghost Parachute, Five South, Gooseberry Pie Lit Magazine* and elsewhere; her science journalism in *National Geographic, Smithsonian, and Audubon.* Kim's stories have been nominated for Pushcart, Best Microfiction, Best Small Fiction, and Best of the Net honors. She was awarded residencies at Storyknife Writers Retreat in 2016 and 2021 and at Dorland Mountain Arts in 2022 and 2023. She holds an MFA from Antioch University - Los Angeles. You can find her on select social media @kimsrogers.

Preparing to be Wrecked

Ronita Chattopadhyay

Viridescent grief

I am in a small wooden boat with two friends. Three friends are in another boat. And you are in the water. I had read about the beautiful, translucent waters of the Umngot River in Dawki in Meghalaya, India. I had seen pictures. We had wondered—do the waters really look that green? Is it because of the underwater plant life? Nothing had suggested that I would also see you.

I am not really surprised though. I have been seeing you in rivers and seas and ponds and mountain streams and swimming pools for so long now. This time, your face is much softer, a little blurred. My friends are arguing passionately about the colour of the river water. They turn to me. I am not sure, I say. Maybe you need to get your eyes checked is what they don't say. I am looking at something else, someone else, is what I don't say. Our small boats make their way to the other side and back.

I want to write about you

but somehow, I end up making a list of all the times I thought of you and missed you. Every time I saw water. Every time I was home in the mountains. Every time I heard Hindi film songs of the 80s and 90s. Every time I came across someone with the same name. At another childhood friend's wedding. Every time I felt I was drowning. Every time I survived.

That first loss

There is something about that first great loss that sticks with you. The first time you realize you cannot keep the people you love safe. It is a slap in the face—a rude, resounding reminder that all your privileges of birth or education or profession can come to naught in an instant. And you are left with a great, big black hole in your stomach that sucks all your energy and will to live. Gradually, you learn to cope and heal in parts. But the grief stays. Sometimes, it feels like a quiet puddle of water gently lapping at your feet. Sometimes, it washes over you, overwhelms you, ravages you like a tsunami. Leaves you undone. The grief stays. And you get on with the business of living.

Even if I want to

We never asked each other questions. We never expected to know the minutiae of each other's lives. Moving across cities and states was overwhelming enough. As roommates, we gave each other space before I knew what giving each other space meant. And then I got the college hostel and you didn't. We always smiled at each other on campus even as our conversations dwindled. Then, we went on very different paths.

I heard that you had begun to withdraw, that you were losing touch with other friends as well. I was perturbed. I thought I should reach out. I didn't. And then another friend called and said, "I have something to tell you. Are you standing? Sit down." I felt an icy hand close around my heart. You had chosen to end your life. Or, maybe, you felt you had no other choice.

I don't know what happened. I can't begin a new habit of asking you questions even if I want to.

Living with the questions

It sounds profound and beautiful when Rilke says it—*To live the questions now. Perhaps you will then gradually, without noticing it, live along some distant day into the answer.*

Did Rilke have to live with these questions:

Should I have done more? Should I have reached out?

Why didn't she tell me? Even if life took us to different continents, why did I have to find she had cancer after she died?

Why did I say *I am busy right now* and *will call back later* and miss the last chance of speaking to him while he was still alive?

Why do good, kind, honest people have to die this way?

Why her?

Why her?

Why her?

Why him?

Preparing to be wrecked

I take off the slippers that have started to thin from all the burdens that my body is carrying. My feet touch the slightly damp, very green grass in this little oasis of colour. I have the sun's warmth for company. Soon, I will head back into the row of tall, dull white buildings in front of me. These buildings that hold both promise and despair. A friend told me that she had read Joan Didion's *The Year of Magical Thinking* after her father had died and that it had wrecked her and also helped her in unexpected ways. And I find myself thinking…should I buy it now as we stumble through these uncertain nights and mornings and this brief, warm afternoon respite?

What I would like to tell ten-year-old me about survival strategies

You have amazing friends at home and school. And you will be blessed with friends later too. Be a witness when they need that and an active participant too. Hold on to them. Some will leave you and this world before their time. And when that time comes, cry as much as you want. For as long as you want. Mourn them however you need to. There is no timeline or script for grief. Any kind of grief.

Don't stop saying hi to that bottlebrush tree you love and the other interesting trees you will meet. Keep making tattoos with silver ferns as long as you can. Maybe, stop trying to taste all the leaves you find. All of them are not going to be tasty or even edible. You don't want the bad surprises that can lead to. And, god knows, there will be enough tragedies in life.

But there will also be a lot of things that bring you joy. Warm sunlight on your face on a winter morning. The quiet luminosity of the moon for company at night. Well…most nights. A ground littered with flowers that are beautiful even after they fall. Books and music and art that will somehow find you at the right time. Friendships and loves that will carry you as much as you carry them.

And try befriending hope and happiness. And keep writing too.

Returning to my favourite place

We used to hold our *dupattas* above our heads, the soft cotton streaming in the wind as we ran down that mountain road. All the girls in the neighbourhood. Just like the way we had seen Hindi film heroines do. And we had our own soundtrack too! It wasn't always very melodious. But it was always very us. There was such simple, unadulterated joy in all that.

I am standing there again. At the top of that road. You are there. I am not surprised.

"How have you been?" you ask. "Not bad," I reply.

"Is my family ok?" you want to know. "I think so. I am not fully sure," I reply.

"Your mother still calls me in December every year for my birthday," I add. I am not sure why. Maybe, that is what you do. Find this communion, this solace, in those who get left behind.

We stand there smiling at each other.

Some things change. Some things remain. The love remains.

Dupatta: a shawl-like scarf traditionally worn by women in India and neighbouring countries

Acknowledgments

"Viridescent Grief" first appeared in *Porch Literary Magazine* Issue 9, October 2024.

"Preparing to be wrecked" first appeared in *Pickle Press Poetry* Issue 1, April 2024

About the Author

Ronita Chattopadhyay (she/her) finds refuge in words. Her work, which almost always seems like poetry to her, has appeared in *The Hooghly Review, Roi Fainéant Press, Akéwì Magazine, streetcake magazine, Setu, Rogue Agent Journal, RIC Journal, Porch Literary Magazine, Dreich, FemAsia,* among others, and anthologies by Querencia Press (*Winter Anthology,* 2024) and Sídhe Press (*To Light The Trails. Poems by Women In a Violent World*). She lives in West Bengal, India, and loves mountains, books and tea.

Memory's Ebb

Kristina Tabor

Perhaps

Before the decline, gifts were Mom's love language. She lit up like a spark when opening new jewelry, putting the earrings or necklace on immediately as if to prove how much it meant to her. Before the decline, she would record the birthday song on your voicemail with the enthusiasm of a marching band. Before the decline, she gave giant hugs when you walked in the door and messy, wet kisses on the cheek. Before the decline, when we pulled away in the car, we'd roll the window down so Isaac, in his child seat, could yell, "Bye bye, Mormor!" frantically waving five tiny fingers, the two of them trying to make eye contact until the very last moment when we turned the corner at the end of the street.

After the decline, she opened gifts with absence in her eyes, sometimes handing them back as if she didn't know what to do with them. After the decline, we had to take away her jewelry because she tried to wear all her rings at once, fingers swollen and green, forcing a visit to the ER to cut the jewelry off. After the decline, she didn't want to hug anymore, pushing us away. After the decline, she wouldn't smile at eight-year-old Isaac, let alone look his way.

Perhaps she could have been a grandmother who threw birthday parties, led the group in song, and kept giving gifts with abandon. Perhaps, in a decade, she could have been a grandmother at Isaac's high school graduation, where she would pull him into her arms and place a wet, sloppy kiss on his almost-college cheek. Perhaps she would have framed a photo of that moment, placed it by her bedside, with its match in his dorm room somewhere. Perhaps, if dementia hadn't taken her down such a steep decline.

Why She Sings

The time she sang a lullaby over your crib, probably "You Are My Sunshine," and you felt her fingers lightly rubbing your back. The time she taught you the words to "Yellow Submarine" because you loved the tune but couldn't read the lyrics on the back of the record yet. The time she sang along to an aria on the classical station coming home from school, and you just wished she'd shut up. The time she sang at the top of her lungs in church, sitting right there next to you, because she said no one could hear her over all those other voices, but you heard her and it was enough to make you turn away. When you realized she had stopped singing the songs she loved because she knew it annoyed you and loved you more. The time she sang in the kitchen when you came home from college after the divorce and realized for the first time she had a beautiful voice. The time she sang "Joy to the World" at the holidays, and your toddler pinched your arm and asked, "Why is Mormor so loud?" so you told him, in an equally audible voice, "She sings because she is happy."

Origin Story

A talented worrier, Mom would suggest a diagnosis of stomach cancer in response to a chronic tummy ache. Her paranoid wonderings made it hard to parse the truth from hyperbole.

This is front-of-mind for me the night she calls, later than normal, saying, "They're going to arrest me."

"Don't be ridiculous," I laugh. My siblings and I learned over a lifetime to treat her exaggerated concerns as a recurring family joke. When she gets a crazy idea in her head, there's no reasoning with her. So, I shrug it off. As I imagine it, Mom is probably sitting in her regular spot at the vinyl-covered kitchen table in her sing-song suburb of Washington, DC. Her neighborhood is a safe haven for suburban families, not a hub of crime.

"No one is going to arrest you, Mom," I say. "What's going on?"

"They told me not to tell you." A pause. Then, crying on the other end. This is alarming. New.

I chew on my lip. Though she is clearly upset, she also makes no sense. I decide to drive to her house to look for clarity.

She opens the door that night slouching in a half-dark hallway, not my normally neatly-donned mother. Her eyes droop like she's aged a decade. She holds her phone in one hand and her wallet in the other, as if unsure what to do with either.

I lead her to the kitchen table, where she puts her head in her hands. "They kept me on the phone all day," she says, going to the bank and taking out money. Then, to the grocery store to buy gift cards. I see her texts, where she sent the gift card codes to an unknown number.

"Why did you do this, Mom?"

"Because I'd be arrested by the IRS if I didn't." The scammers' lie.

They continue to text her while I'm there, until I take over, saying that I called the police. I phone her banks, her credit card company, and file a police report. None of this lifts the new sag on my mother's face, betraying exhaustion, confusion, and terror. All I can do is make her a cup of tea and put her to bed.

Rather than falling in the category of "one of Mom's exaggerations," this incident would be filed under "evidence Mom has dementia." Other cases include being chronically, almost absurdly late to dates, frequently forgetting her wallet or purse; and leaving the oven on, once charring chicken thighs in their own fat, fortunately not catching on fire.

It's nearly midnight when I leave. She asks again, a renewed fear in her eyes, "Are they going to arrest me?"

"Don't be ridiculous. No one is going to arrest you."

I say it gently. I do not laugh this time.

Broken Record

Mom texts after ten, then again at two in the morning. I receive the messages at 6 am, awake when my young son starts to run hurdles in his bedroom, hopping from chair to bed to floor, his own personal obstacle course.

"The TV isn't working again."

"The TV is broken," she repeats.

If I call back too early, if she hasn't misplaced her phone, she'll scold me for waking her up. So I wait.

My son makes it to the bus stop on time, and I take two work meetings before I get another text.

"When are you coming over. The TV is broken."

It's not a question. She rarely asks questions anymore. Born and raised a Brit, politeness was once a hallmark of her personality. Now, these commands are a permitted impropriety because, although she still lives in her house independently, she is not fully of sound mind. I will help her. There is no question of it.

During a break between meetings, I call her.

"My TV is broken," she says immediately when picking up. No "Hello, how are you." Perhaps she doesn't remember the text messages.

"I know, Mom. It's probably the remote again."

"When are you coming over to help."

"I can't come over today." In addition to my full-time job and having a son under the age of ten, we live a twenty-minute drive away. "I'll come by this weekend."

"Okay." Then, silence. Among other things she's forgotten is how to say goodbye, how to get off a phone call.

In the quiet, I imagine the echoes in her mind. A manic chorus of "The TV is broken. Broken. The TV is broken. The TV is broken." Sometimes she paces the house. I've seen it on FaceTime: she's in the dark, light of the phone casting a pall around her eyes, nothing moving but the ceiling. She's circling, circling, circling.

"I love you, Mom."

"I love you too." Some proprieties continue on autopilot.

In the silence, I imagine that her mind grinds, spins on the other end of the line.

"I'll talk to you later." And I hang up.

I drive to pick up my son from aftercare when my phone buzzes.

"The TV is broken."

Another text. "When are you coming over."

"When are you coming over."

Mom Learns She Is Unfit to Drive a Car

The decision is baffling. She spent decades shuttling four children to and fro, here and there. Pretty much everywhere they wanted to be. High school carpool or jazz band practice or swim team. Apparently, a doctor ordered this driving test. She doesn't believe it. But still, she gives it her best effort.

Mom first learned to drive in England where she grew up. Stick shift, left side of the road. The States spoiled her with automatic transmission, unleaded fuel, right-side driving. Still, she never forgot the rules of the motorway back home. Driving a rental between Heathrow and the house where she was born, she orated to the backseat, recounting epic European car vacations she took as a kid. Sometimes they'd drive on the right side of the road, take pit stops that were just a hole in the ground. No! Not even a toilet! Vistas memorialized in silver photos, now boxed away.

She remembers her father drove on those trips. It's funny what Mom remembers and what she forgets. Her mother never learned to drive in the first place. Post-war, she made a home, a family. Why get a license? He shuttled her everywhere in their VW Bug. After Parkinsons took him, minicabs brought her to Waitrose.

But for Mom, when her kids grew up, the car became her escape: power under the pedal, the dream of speeding away in a cloud of dust, away from all the cooking, the cleaning, the husband screaming, the ironing, even his underwear. She remembers that: following in her mother's domestic footsteps.

Unlike her mother, she eventually divorced. Proved that she could live on her own. Bought herself new cars whenever it felt right. Like a new, hybrid Honda CRV, lily white with big GBR and Union Jack bumper stickers that showed she owned this thing. Her children had disliked the car, the new grand piano, the diamond earrings. But couldn't she treat herself every now and then, just live her life, goddamn it?

Her last ride behind the wheel happens in the driving school's car, with a chaperone. The instructor is poised to hit the brakes when things go wrong.

And it all goes wrong. She misses traffic signals, road markings, pedestrians. "It's so distressing," she says when she fails. She wants to go to the store the next day and wonders who took the CRV from the garage.

Almost daily, Mom emails her children with the subject line "Memories." One click opens pictures from before dementia took over. She hugs the grandkids who she once buckled into child seats, whose hands she held while crossing the street, whose names she sometimes forgets now. She smiles at the camera, memorializing another time, unknowing of everything she will one day forget.

Shrine of Broken Logic

Mom carries nail scissors and a bundle of rawhide. Dehydrated chicken snakes up the finger-length sticks like suffocating vines, and she cuts it away— snip snip—with the persistence of a mosquito bite scraped by the edge of a fingernail—scratch scratch—until it sheds onto the floor. She does this like a stage play, acting like no one is watching. But I'm there, an audience of one, just on the other side of the coffee table. I vacillate between disgust and relief that her dementia isn't making her do something worse, that she's still able to take herself to the bathroom, can still feed herself breakfast, lunch, and dinner.

She prunes the rawhides for Teddy, the dog she adopted the year things got bad, the year her partner died unexpectedly, the same year her little black dog passed away. This time she got a little white dog, which she saw as a good sign. An omen of better things. I saw an animal afraid of his own shadow. A rescue, as if it explained the growling, lunging at children, nipping at me, defecating all over the carpet.

Now the dog curls in her lap in the space where her babies once swam. She strokes him like a pregnant belly, protective. "Why are you cutting all this rawhide, Mom?" I ask.

"He won't eat dog food," she says. "I'm worried he'll starve." This is the irrationality that comes with dementia.

Growing up, Mom would prepare me an after-school snack: a slice of American cheese, Goldfish crackers, cut up apple, and a spoonful of peanut butter while I watched afternoon cartoons. Today, she does this for the dog, as if a child: snippings sprinkled over days-old cooked meat, cheddar cheese, and other layered droppings. In those days, I devoured my food; licking every last layer of peanut butter until my tongue tasted the metallic spoon. Now, Teddy doesn't touch it.

One day, when I come by to refill her medications, I find Mom on the sofa surrounded by her shreddings, layered like a powdering of snow. Dried meat, scattered everywhere, is her offering at the shrine to broken logic.

When asked, she shrugs wanly, reacting only when I take away the rawhide, vacuum the shavings. "But what will he eat?" she says.

She isn't so far gone to realize that the promise of the white dog has proven a false prophecy. "He's a very bad boy," she says. It's true: he's untrainable, aggressive, loved by only her. She, too, will reach that point someday in the near future. Logic will disappear, replaced by bitterness, and loved by only those of us left with patience. Will I too make a shrine to her odd delights, nurture bizarre culinary preferences, stroke her hair with her head in my lap, and when someone questions these oddities, wonder: "But what will she eat?"

Runestones

The first time you push Mom's hospital wheelchair, there's a panic that comes with so many unknowns. How will you navigate to the parking lot with the wheelchair? You see the sliding doors ahead, relieved you won't need anyone's help to prop the door. Then, how will you get her from the wheelchair and into the car with nothing but your meager muscle? You anticipate the awkward intimacy of buckling a grown woman into her car seat, next to the booster for your small son.

You push these realities aside and instead search for comfort in symbols, looking for a sign. You find runes in the part of her many-toned strands of silver hair. Her scalp is a river diverging in gray waves, curving from a bed of bare pink skin. The lines carve a channel, forming an ancient, divine language. For a few seconds, you get lost in wondering what they foretell. You feel comfort that this magic might do all the knowing for you, a reassuring companion in the opaque storm of Mom's dementia.

Something quiet, maybe the buzz of the hospital's fluorescent lights or the hum of the doors opening and closing, nudges you back to the moment. You look, again, at her hair. If these lines are carvings, they foretell nothing you don't already know: Mom's decline is deepening.

Later, you will learn that runes were Odin's language, used by Danes and Swedes to memorialize the dead on runestones, as if an etching could harness the fleeting wildness that is memory into permanence.

Swallow

Mom loved Brie, creamy soft chunks sandwiched with rind, paired with the crusty end of the baguette. Strawberries, quartered and sprinkled with sugar. Roast pork with crispy rinds and candied yams for Christmas.

Now, at the age of seventy, the doctor says she must stop eating solid food. After two unsuccessful surgeries, her esophagus is broken. I'm there, as I am at all doctor's appointments, because Mom has dementia and can't care for herself. They also find saliva in her lungs—a sign that she's forgetting how to swallow. This dysphagia could kill her, as it does half of all dementia patients.

§

When my son was born, my milk didn't come in. He wouldn't latch. All I wanted was to feed him, but my body didn't cooperate. I went to a lactation consultant. I pumped every last drop out of my aching breasts. I paid for the real stuff: milk from a milk bank, expressed by other mothers. It was an exhausting, expensive, depressing time. After weeks, I switched to formula.

And yet, Mom asked at the time: "Shouldn't you try again? I'm sure he'll latch soon." She had four kids and couldn't fathom being unable to do such a simple thing as breastfeeding.

§

After the appointment, I bring her some soup. She looks at the spoon and says, "What's this for?" She clumsily opens the plastic top, the broth breaching the brim of the clear quart container. I clean the spill because it seems like the only concrete thing I can fix in that moment of shock, the first time she forgets how to feed herself.

§

A favorite video shows me feeding my son a bottle of formula. He makes little sucking noises, the sound of a baby eating, swallowing, nourished. In that video, I look so happy, rested, and in love with my boy.

Now my son is older, he feeds himself. He loves mashed potatoes, french fries, instant oatmeal with little sugared dinosaur eggs. He pulls over a stepstool to the kitchen cabinet and grabs himself a small bowl for dessert after he's cleaned his plate. It is a wonder that this is the same child who was once just over five pounds, cradled in my arms, sucking from a bottle.

§

Although my son couldn't latch as an infant, he always knew how to suck, how to swallow. Not all babies are as fortunate; my mother's condition—dysphasia—is common in small children, too. To treat it, adults and kids alike have to adjust their diet, get therapy to ingest food differently, tip their head, move their tongue. Babies have the advantage: they can still learn, brains like little sponges. Dementia makes the brain like a sponge run dry, corners breaking off, crevices molding.

For Mom, therapy, unremembered, doesn't take.

Dementia's Orphans

Six sets of plants and cut flowers surround my mother in varying stages of life and decay. She sits in silence while I help the movers inventory her things. A ficus holds on to the north-facing window. A poinsettia in red foil hasn't moved since Christmas, and its curled, dried leaves litter the floor. Standing water smells rank in the iris bowl. Bulbs pop out of a wood planter, packed with straw, supposed to foster new spring growth. Instead it's swampy—she watered it, forgot, then watered it again, and again and again.

Like these plants, my mother's mind wilts, molds, droops. First, little things—dates and times—slipped her mind. She fell victim to fraud. She lost words, and without language, she stopped engaging with friends and family. She forgot how to plug in the blender and how to turn off the oven. She failed a driving test.

Now, movers measure the furniture to see if it will fit in her new apartment at the care home. "This?" they say, pointing to a four decade-old lamp with moth holes in the shade. "This?" to a CD tower, untouched in years. "This? This is a good piece of furniture," they point to the teak dining room table.

"Let's try to take as much of it as we can," I say. Mom sits on the couch, cheeks sagging, biting skin off her fingers. When I hug her, she leans in with her head on my stomach, and then she abruptly pushes me away.

The movers don't notice the burst of anger. One of them points: "This ficus is a good, hardy plant." Its spindly, six-foot branches drink in the suburban sun in the same place it's sat for decades. "We see this all the time: orphan plants," they say. Pots that can't possibly move to a space with three windows instead of twelve. Plants that are easier to throw in the dumpster than stack in a moving truck. "It's sad," they say, "to see these thriving, living things left behind." The movers adopt them, give them a new home and attention. They bring them back to life.

Before my mother forgot how to use her email, she regularly sent me notes titled "Memories," with no message, just photos from years past. These images showed her holding her grandchildren with a recognition and love unseen now for years. The Christmas cactus bloomed pink in the background. Fresh cut lilies extended their stamen, perfuming the room. Echoes from the past: the smiles, the smell, the growth and bloom.

Now, Mom moves to a home with professional caretakers who understand age and infirmity. She should have everything she needs, activities, amenities, companions. I bring plastic and polyester peonies to warm her new apartment, arrange the stems in a crystal vase, set it on the sill. The next time I visit, I catch her watering them. She won't say "I love you" before I leave. But all of us are resilient, despite Mom's forgetting.

Visiting Hours

A kind-faced greeter helps direct foot traffic, sorting patients and visitors alike by ailment and destination, whether ER or maternity ward or, like me, otherwise. Framed reproductions and snippets of scripture dot the hospital's broad, bright walls. Fluorescent yellow bounces off the polished linoleum floors, shining between scuffs from the morning's traffic.

I turn towards the "Elevators This Way" sign, imagining a well-worn rut where I've walked daily since Mom's hospitalization. Here are the route's landmarks: the security guard on the left inspecting visitor badges; the gaggle of nurses on their break, sitting by the window like plants yearning for natural light; a silent piano in the corner, beckoning for someone to tinkle its keys. Everywhere, the stale smell of internal circulation, cut only by occasional opening and closing of sliding doors.

At the elevators, I hit 3, followed closely by someone in a wheelchair. Before I see her, I assume she is an elderly, infirm person, like the one I'm visiting. Instead, her sweaty soccer jersey and racer-stripe shorts betray adolescence. Dirty perspiration mats her hair. Blood trickles down her shin. A woman wearing scrubs pushes the wheelchair, hits 2 for the emergency room, and angles the girl to face me. I wonder where her mother is. A grimace etches pain in deep-set lines of a young, unwashed face. Her body contorts like it's trying to spare itself, and I think it's too early in her life to intimate how the body renders itself fallible.

The nurse pushes off when the elevator hits 2, and I brace myself for 3, where Mom lies. She is bedridden, riddled with dementia, eyes unknowing who they see. She is unprompted by my face. Not even the simple first and last name, visible on the visitor's badge, emblazoned on my shirt, offers a memory.

Though I am a stranger to her, she lets me hold her hand. It's this I will remember fondly on what's our last trip to the hospital: her pale, blue-veined knuckles, and a palm so warm that it's hard to believe it will go cold within days. Hers is less wrinkled, twenty years younger, than her mother's was at the end. Cuticles are nibbled down to a quick, lacerated and caked with dried blood from nervous biting like chewed pencil-ends at the bottom of a much-carried purse.

I smooth her hair when she retches, shush her like a child. Did the soccer player's mother show up at the ER, I wonder? Did the broken bone reset in her leg, and will it always nag at her when it rains? I want to ask the nurses on break when I walk out of the building. They continue to lean by the window, now smattered with evening rain. The piano is a still life, untouched. Dusk blankets outside the sliding doors with a sky in strands of pink and almost orange weaving in pale clouds, like fingers curling through the waning blue, holding onto the last light.

Shells

Mom, you raised me, made every meal, drove me to school, put me to bed every night. You would never, ever leave the room or put down the phone without saying "I love you" one more time. Your devotion to your children and grandchildren was fierce. Then, dementia took everything from you: your personality, perspective, ability to communicate.

You knew that I always struggled with depression, but because mental illness was taboo when you grew up, we didn't talk about it. You would have been mortified to know that your dementia pulled me deeper into hopelessness. I couldn't sleep. I overate and gained weight. I suffered panic attacks. Depression felt insurmountable.

Most times in crisis, I have done something drastic—cut all my hair off or moved to another state. This time, I would travel somewhere new: Costa Rica, which felt impossibly far away after years at home in a pandemic, after years watching you decline.

Because of your dementia, you never asked to see my photos, which once had been a requirement of all your kids returning from a trip. So let me tell you: I was surrounded by rainforest, black sand beaches, howler monkeys, mango trees. I spent most days doing nothing but write or nap in the 100 degrees. Yes, the beaches were black! I buried my toes in that sand, watched pelicans dive for fish, laughed at two golden retrievers bounding in tandem down the shore.

One morning, before the sun reached its peak, I found an endless bank of tiny seashells blanketing the bank, glinting like jewels, and glistening from a soak in the Pacific Ocean. Each was remarkable in shape, pattern, and color, these riches dotting the ocean's edge. I crouched, mesmerized by the spiral of this one or the black-pocked royal purple of that one. Some of the shells skittered off on little legs. Others basked in the not-nearly-noon light and a salt water rinse.

Mom, in this Costa Rican trove of shells on a ray-drenched morning, I discovered a small opening, a simple joy to crack depression's darkness. And

I wondered: What other minute things had I overlooked in this undertow of feeling? In the pain of witnessing you lose your mind, what memories had I, too, forgotten, ones that would make me too sad, ones that felt so very far away from this stranger you had become today. Like how you always insisted on one last kiss and one last hug, even when I was so over it as a teenager. How every time we came back from being out of town, you would meet us at the airport. How you squeezed my hand with reassurance at all the right times.

Mom, these thoughts of you take on a unique shape and color and curve. They settle on the edge of my banks of memory, where depression, like the ocean, will always ebb. Your soul, when whole, was as remarkable as the trove of shells on a Costa Rican beach.

Acknowledgements

Thank you to the literary journals that first published the following stories:

"Why She Sings," *LEON Literary Review*

"Mom Learns She Is Unfit to Drive a Car," *Twin Pies Literary*

"Dementia's Orphans," *Superstition Review*

About the Author

Kristina Tabor (she/her) writes short fiction and nonfiction. Her work appears in Best Microfiction 2023 and many literary journals. She has an MFA from Randolph College and lives in the Washington, DC, area.

The Doctor

Janet Murie

The Eldest Daughter 2024

My father was a residential school doctor.

The Mother 1957

There is a photograph of my mother from when she was a young woman. She is wearing a blue skirt and short matching jacket, nipped tight at the waist with a thin leather belt, and blue high heels. The suit was homemade and the closest a small-town girl from Ontario could get to Dior's New Look. She is holding a 2-week-old baby and standing next to an airplane with pontoons and propellers, waiting to board the three-hour flight from Trenton, Ontario to Norway House, Manitoba.

(Norway House is a small settlement north of Lake Winnipeg and is part of the Cree Nation. If you look it up on Wikipedia, you won't find any reference to the Cree people who had lived there for centuries. Instead, you will find a reference to the Norwegian convicts who built a road through the Cree territory on behalf of the Hudson's Bay Company.)

It was one of those humid June days in Southern Ontario. The scent of a lilac hedge half a mile away carried and the sky was hazy. She licked her fingers to try to flatten her hair, which was starting to frizz. She hadn't seen her husband in six weeks, when she flew out to give birth to her first child.

With a brand-new baby, this young woman was returning to a remote community where there were few women who spoke the language she did. She would be alone with the baby for weeks at a time while her husband travelled from outpost to outpost across the Eastern Arctic. She would keep a garden, bake bread, and take care of her small family. She couldn't wait to start this first true adventure of her life.

Someone helped her board the plane. She settled into her seat—one of nine—lay the baby down beside her and reached into her bag for a thermos. She poured herself a martini, lit a cigarette, and stared out the window as the propellers started to spin.

The Physician, The Healer 1957

"I am not indifferent.

"I have said this before—everything we have done is for the good of everyone, even those people who are so ungrateful. I am not indifferent and know it will be hard for a while, but it is all for the best.

"Maybe it looks harsh, these people in the boat, the woman with the child in a tikanagan on her back. I see the look on her face. We had to load them from a cargo loader. It didn't mean anything. It was just the easiest way. They didn't want to go.

"Even though they were going to civilization they still wore their filthy parkas, didn't bother to clean their children. Don't they know we will help them, teach them English, tame their dogs, show them there is a merciful God, send them to school, TB hospitals?

"We are sending a nurse with them. I'm going as well, and the sailors will make sure no one is unruly. They rarely are, those people. They can stare a hole right through you but rarely act up.

"We tagged everyone in the boats to keep track of them. I've taken some pictures for the historical record—you can see the tags here, with their destinations and government numbers. Not much point in adding names, we can't say them and are going to give them English ones once they get wherever they're going.

"I felt badly when we had to cull the dogs in that village. I thought that people were going to go mad, but the dogs were a threat to public health. There was one man, in particular, the RCMP had to restrain him. It's not like he saw them shoot his dogs. They took them out back."

The Things circa 1957 i

There are things I wish I did not own.

Mukluk: 1:a sealskin or reindeer-skin boot typically worn by indigenous peoples of usually arctic regions of Alaska, Canada, Greenland, and eastern Siberia.[1]

When my family left Moose Factory for Ottawa, we brought half a dozen pairs of beaded mukluks. They were moosehide with fur trim, elaborate embroidery, and intricate beading. When we left Ottawa for British Columbia, where my father ran a TB hospital that used to be a residential school, I wore the mukluks when it snowed. They were the most exotic thing I had ever seen and when I wore them, I believed I had been kidnapped from Romanian royalty who were searching for me and would take me home. But they were only ever intended for dry snow, not the wet snow in western Canada. The boots got wet and hardened and were thrown away.

I often wonder why I was allowed to wear them in wet weather. Maybe they didn't know.

Sealskin doll. The oldest dolls found in Canada were made by the ancestors of the Inuit living at Brooman Point, on Bathurst Island, about a thousand years ago. The Inuit have inhabited the Arctic for at least two thousand years. We do not know at what point in their history they began making dolls, but it is certainly an ancient tradition.[2]

I had a sealskin doll from childhood, a foot tall with an embroidered face and soft boots. I would bury my face in it and breathe in the gamey smell. It moved with me many times—when I left my parents' home, full of grief and rage, I took it with me. Then it came along on all the impulsive moves I made in my twenties, and on into my thirties and forties. I took it with me

1   Wikipedia

2   Wikipedia

to Toronto when I turned fifty. That was when I noticed one foot was falling off. I called some museums to find someone to restore it with no luck.

It became infested with moths.

The Eldest Daughter 2024

I recently learned of the discovery of 96 bodies beneath the property I grew up on that was part of Sto:lo Nation.

Nine. I was nine when we moved there. The property felt massive to a child, although it would be large by any measure. There was the house, a large rose garden, and an orchard, and my sister and I rarely left this area. I can't remember if we had been told not to wander or just preferred not to.

Then there was the enormous lot the hospital sat on, imposing and ominous, red brick. I never went inside, or even close to the front doors. Behind the hospital were residences for the doctors, small houses like army barracks.

The house was out of a storybook, with an attic, a root cellar, places I was sure held some kind of secret. But no matter how often I went back to check they were always empty, scrubbed of whatever treasures they might have held.

The storybooks lied.

The house had two living rooms and a small, dark dining room where we often sat in silent misery for shared meals.

The only time we saw other doctors was at my parents' Christmas cocktail parties. Doctors would come with wives in their fur coats. I loved the smell of those coats, earthy and warm. I claimed the job of carrying them upstairs and laying them on my parent's bed. Sometimes I would bury myself beneath the coats to better breathe them in.

It is odd you can't Google my father. It's like he never existed, never worked for the Canadian government. He was a mid-level bureaucrat, but prominent enough that one year Who's Who in Canada sent him an application. He filled it out in the dog's name and sent it back. He said it was bullshit but still talked about it a lot. Still, you'd think there would be at least a single reference to him on the internet. I can't even find his obituary.

We were afraid of him. He would come home full of rage after the short walk across the lawn, as if something that had happened that day was our fault.

Of course I didn't know what it meant, how it appeared, where we lived. I know what it means now. I don't even know if my mother knew. He never said a word about it until decades later, in the 1980s, when the first public stories started coming out. He said "nobody ever told me about abuse. There was no abuse." Definite and furious.

When we played, we biked, we hid, we ran, we never knew that there were bodies buried under the grass beneath our feet, 96 of them.

Decades later when they tore the house down, I thought it was disrespectful. Now I understand that it is a sin that it ever existed.

The Things circa 1957 ii

Soapstone carvings: Contrary to popular belief, most Inuit carvings are not in soapstone but in harder stone such as chrysotile, olivine, chlorite, serpentine, or peridotite. Even granite and quartz are used occasionally. Finding a continuing source of good carving stone has been a long-standing problem for many Arctic communities. The problem has become accentuated in the last decade or so. In some cases, communities have turned to imported stone. Some carvers have even begun using marble, often coloured black with shoe polish.[3]

My father bought soapstone carvings during his time in the Arctic—a beautiful pair of jade-green walruses, two hunters heavy and squat, and a bone-coloured small figure of a man walking. There was also an oil pan, but I don't know where it is now.

We played with them as children, pulling the tusks from the walruses (they slid easily in and out of slots on the faces) and the spears from the hunters. The stone cool and smooth.

To this day they live on bookshelves (my place) or knickknack shelves (with my sister). On mine they have poetry books on either side, at my sister they live with the Royal Doulton.

Cree beading and embroidery. Swampy Cree and Ojibway beadwork and embroidery ... are some of the most beautiful artifacts in the Thunder Bay Museum's collections. Pouches, patches, belts, bags sashes and aprons form the bulk of the holdings, but some pieces are as big as table clothes. Most of these items were collected by one man, Anglican Archdeacon Richard Faries who, from 1899 to about 1950, was a missionary to the Cree Indians in a large region centred on York Factory on Hudson Bay. In payment for services such as medical care, baptisms and marriages, Faries collected the beadwork and embroidery done by the local women.[4]

My mom had some special things tucked away in her cedar dresser—

3   Canada.ca

4   Thunder Bay Museum

beaded belts, necklaces, an embroidered belt. I hoped to return these with the tikanagan but gave them to a complicated boyfriend with a connection to Indigenous communities in B.C., thinking he would find someone who would love them. He told me he was going to sell them to fund political action. I wanted these things to find their way home. He returned them when I asked.

The Mother 1971

In between the angry words that would make their way unimpeded upstairs to my room and the even more threatening silences, my mother would try to make happy moments. Sometimes she would make taffy, the old-fashioned kind that was full of molasses and you had to boil it and then pull it once it was cool enough, but not so cool that it got hard. This was a finer line than I am making it sound. Pulling taffy was something unique to me and my mother. Both the doctor and my sister were excluded from this process, and none of us ever ate it.

But there was something about the pulling. We had an old house, and the kitchen was the biggest room. It was papered with yellows and oranges and whites, ridiculously cheerful for how unhappy the house always felt. The kitchen itself felt empty, cabinets and fridge and stove pushed up against the four walls and that wallpaper couldn't do a thing to cheer it up. But there was a lot of empty space to pull taffy. And pull we would, laughing as the taffy stretched out and we would have to run towards each other when it got too thin and threatened to hit the floor.

There was something defining about this back and forth with my mother. When I was very young, I would help her fold sheets after she ironed, grabbing my corners and running towards her, grabbing the new corners and dashing backwards across the empty space. It didn't end until her death, this coming closer then moving away again.

The Eldest Daughter 2024

When I learned of the bodies at my childhood home, I launched a search that hasn't yet ended. I have learned that searches are complicated things with their own set of rules, and often what you think you are looking for quickly shifts into something else that was there all along, you just didn't know it.

To find what is lost you need to get your bearings.
Where are you on this earth? What is your purpose here?
Which parts of this story will be yours to tell after all is said, and finally done, and which parts will belong to the lost? If the lost is not part of you?

To find what is lost, you need to know what it is.
But I don't know if the things I seek were ever truly known to me.

To find what is lost, gather a team to help you.
Phone your oldest friend, the only one who has been to that house.
"They found bodies there, at Coqualeetza. Did you hear?"
Then listen to the long silence that comes back to you.
"Did you hear what I said?"
"I heard you."
The quiet will tell you that this is not the person to join you on this journey. At this time, in this place, for this particular kind of search.

Know that memories will come unbidden and unwanted. Once you open the gate for them, they will come. But they will come angry and sad and uncontrollable. You will remember swinging high on the wooden swing and imagining your real family, the one that left you with these strangers. You will remember your sister chasing you around the rose bed, the thing the doctor was most proud of, with live worms. You will remember sheltering from family fights under the covers with a book and a flashlight, and the time you hit a neighbour for no reason other than your own sadness.

None of these are the things you went looking for.

The Things circa 1957 iii

Tikanagan: Among some Algonquian (sic) peoples: a baby carrier and cradle made from a thin, rectangular board (to which the baby is strapped) with a support for the baby's feet and (typically) a wooden bow to protect its head. A tikinagan can be carried on one's back or placed somewhere with the baby in an upright position.[5]

I have a tikanagan that is painted forest green and has a padded pouch for a baby. The embroidered blankets are still intact, although the wood is beginning to split. There is a picture of my mother carrying my sister on her back, my sister's small round face peering out at the camera with her dark, dark eyes.

I have carried this with me since my mother died fifteen years ago. Once I called the Norway House Cree Nation and explained to someone that I hoped to return this tikanagan. When I described it, the woman I spoke with said, "Oh, my auntie might have done the embroidery." I said I would pack it up and send it back, but it is a complicated shape to pack, and I couldn't figure out how to do it. Then I thought maybe I could drive it up there, and a friend said she would go with me, but we didn't and now I am on the other side of the country, still with the tikanagan. Even when I can't see it, I know it is there.

Friends cannot understand why I wouldn't just give it to a museum, and I don't know how to explain it.

The Physician, The Healer 1946

John had gone to medical school on the GI Bill. His family didn't have money and it was his only way in. He was smart enough to graduate high school but not smart enough for a scholarship. Did he have fun at university? I think he had friends then, just not later. There is a family legend about a time John went to a pub—this was after he came back from the war, damaged beyond recognition—and his father physically hauled him home. None of us ever asked for more of this story with so much of it left untold.

In 1939 he lied about his age and joined the army. All the time I knew him he was haunted by his time in the infantry. He had medals tucked away under his socks and underwear, but we never knew what they were for. He refused to answer questions about it. The haunting showed in the way he jumped at loud noises, was angered by anything unexpected.

He thought he might have been happier without a family, living alone and working as a doctor for the Peace Corps even though he hated to travel. I know this because he said so, more than once. No one ever asked him why he didn't want us, it seemed obvious, and this might have been the same kind of romantic idea as living at the YWCA—not really knowing what it would look like but feeling good to say and to picture. Out in the world doing good with no complicating personal relationships to navigate, or make you feel bad about yourself.

When he would travel for work my mom and sister and I would eat sandwiches for dinner in front of the tv, then watch a movie and throw popcorn for the dog. There were no fights. No threats or insults. No fists. I spent my time downstairs instead of hiding in my room with a stack of books. I could have a friend over with no fear of some kind of scene that would result in them being sent home in tears.

And what would this Peace Corps dream have meant for the others, for the people he traveled to outposts and residential schools to see? Just a different person to harm them, I expect. There would always have been someone else to scoop them up and send them to homes in the city, away from their families. Someone else to give them sugar water while telling them it was vitamins and then waiting to see how it affected their health. Someone else to turn a blind eye to what was being done in residential schools.

I have friends who tell me they don't believe in the sins of the father. But I do. I always have.

6b In Canada in the 1940s and 1950s, experiments with nutritional supplements were conducted on Indigenous children. This happened at the direction of the Canadian government.[6]

---

6   CBC

The Physician, The Healer 1984

What has not been told?

"We weren't to tell anyone, but so few of us are left I suppose it won't matter now. I have not told you—I have not told anyone—that I was one of the doctors administering vitamins to Indians all that time ago. Some got supplements and some didn't. No one knew. They all thought the supplements would prevent tuberculosis, which was ravaging the Indians then. We weren't sure of the connection and there was no other way to find out.

"What? No. Of course we couldn't tell them. It was a secret.

"We also cut off dental care to see if that would make a difference. We didn't know.

"It was impossible to communicate with those people, they didn't speak English. They lived in shacks and didn't care to improve their lives. Why are people mad about this now? Everything we did was for their betterment."

How should I begin?

"I can't explain this to people now. What's done is done, and we thought it was for the best. We thought we were helping. Sometimes people suffer while you figure things out. That's how it works.

"I was just doing what I was told to do. You have to understand. It was different then. You weren't there, you can't possibly know."

What have you lied about?

"Is omission a lie? Or is it a lie if I say something because I don't know otherwise? If so, I suppose there were lies. But it was for their own good. We were just trying to help, make it easier for them to fit in. Get them into civilization. They thought they didn't want it, but it was for the best. When that politician said he wanted to "kill the Indian in the child," it wasn't a bad thing. It was all for them.

"I do know this—in all my years there, no one told me about abuse. There was no abuse."

Mother and Eldest Daughter 1994

Barbara knew her way around Chinatown. Every Christmas our stockings were full of things she found in the nooks and crannies of dark, narrow stores that smelled of incense. Tiny ceramic bowls that I would line up on my windowsill, something I do to this day. Chopsticks no one could use, in deeply saturated jewel tones. Silly wind-up toys that we still recycle, even though they stopped working decades ago. Incense without incense burners.

So her current errand was easy. She handed over her credit card and said no to the receipt—she had had her expenditures questioned for the last time. Each purchase was wrapped carefully in tissue paper and placed in a plastic bag. She got into her twenty-five-year-old Buick and drove slowly home, stopping carefully at each stop sign.

"I never break the law," she would say proudly.

"What about Rosa Parks?" I would ask and she would say "the law is the law" and I would exhale loudly through my nose.

Even though my father was a doctor, he didn't trust dentists. And that mistrust extended to basic oral hygiene like flossing and brushing twice a day. So by the time he was sixty he had the minimum number of teeth you need to chew food. His smile was gappy.

"Your father doesn't look like a physician," a nurse friend said to me.

And it was true. He would wear a $2000 dollar suit, a bespoke shirt, Ferragamo shoes, a silk ascot (!!), and still have that toothless smile. Jesus Christ.

Periodically my mother would suggest dentures.

"I'll spend all that money and die two weeks later," he would say. Money was not a concern. He just didn't want to go to the dentist. But eventually he gave in.

He died two weeks later.

Not of the heart attack we all had been expecting for years—he'd had five– but he fell down the stairs and hit his head.

He had insisted that there be no funeral, no doubt imagining people getting up and making up nice things to say about him. So the family met in the back room of a funeral home, said a few unkind things, collected his ashes and went home.

A few days later I popped in to have dinner with mom. She said she would talk to him and sometimes yell at him. I asked where he was, and she pointed at the bookcase. She had cleared off one shelf for the plain, faux-wood urn.

I took a closer look. "Mom, are those stones?" I thought she had selected stones from the garden to surround the urn. It seemed unusually sentimental.

She walked over and wound up each one of the wind-up hopping teeth she had brought home from Chinatown. We both watched in silence for a second before starting to laugh.

Three years later the last residential school in Canada closed.

Epilogue, September 18, 2024

The Canadian Medical Association formally apologized for harm to Indigenous communities.

About the Author

Janet Murie has the good fortune to live on the unceded territory of the Cowichan people on Vancouver Island, and spends time writing, avoiding writing, and watching for wildlife from her home in the woods.